RUBY SMILES

By Prudence Williams
Illustrated by Patrick Carlson

Copyright © 2020 by Prudence Williams Shipman

All Rights reserved

No part of this work may be reproduced or transmitted in any form or by any means, electronic or mechanical, including photocopying and recording, or by any information storage or retrieval system without the prior written permission of Team Shipman Publishing unless such copying is expressly permitted by federal copyright law. Address inquires to Team Shipman Publishing, P.O. Box 1244 Stockbridge, GA 30281

Hi! I'm Ruby!

When Ruby hears the alarm sound in the morning, she smiles! It's a new day and she has a lot to do!

She waits for Mr. Shipman to come out. She runs in circles and wishes him a good morning! She's happy to see him, excited to start a new day.

Bathroom! Bathroom! She rushes Mr. Shipman to the door! Gotta go! Gotta go! She runs outside and takes care of business and say hi to the cat on her way down the stairs. What a great day! Look at the sun coming up! Ruby smiles, and knows things are going to go her way!

Ruby smiles when Mr. Shipman brings her breakfast out in a big ole bowl! Oh boy! Oh boy! She smiles as she discovers a special meaty treat Mr. Shipman gave her today!

After she eats, Ruby smiles and settles in for a great day of play. When Mr. Shipman leaves for work, Ruby grins and thinks… today I've got so much to do! I've got to watch over the house, take a nap, play in the leaves, take a nap, bark at the frogs by the pond, take a nap, and teach the cat a thing or two!

Ruby smiles when she sees Mr. Shipman come home from work! She runs up and dances when he walks in the door!

Boy, has she missed him today! She goes and greets him, smiling and wagging her tail, all the way!

Ruby smiles when Mr. Shipman sits on the deck and lets her play with her pet squirrels who live in the backyard trees. They love when she chases them and races around behind them. They run and run and run and run, up and down the branches and trees. Ruby barks and chases them, but never catches them because she knows that would hurt them, and she would never do that!

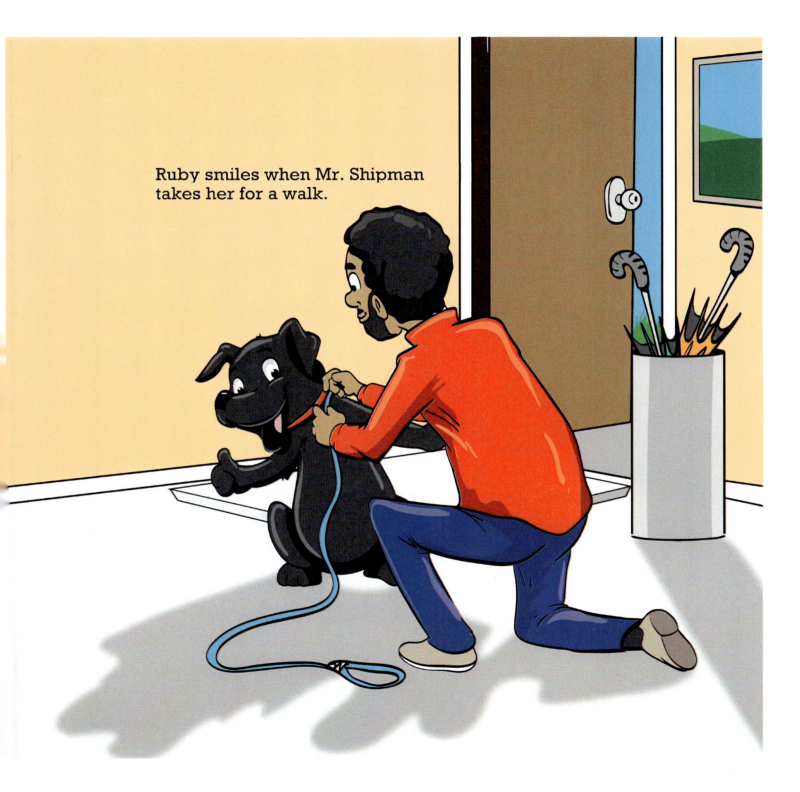
Ruby smiles when Mr. Shipman takes her for a walk.

She likes her bright red leash! She knows she looks like a superstar walking down the street. She can't wait for the kids in the neighborhood to come and talk to her and play with her. She knows all their names. There's Zaire, Khalil, Je'Rontai, Corey, Cobey, Camron, Teryn, Jada, Shermarke, Taniya, Jaylei, Jahari, Kieran, and BJ . They love her and she loves them, and she smiles for each and every one of them!

Ruby smiles when she and Mr. Shipman get home! Whew! That was a long walk, and now she's thirsty. Mr. Shipman gives her water, and Ruby smiles when he puts ice in it too! UMMMMM! So cool and good! "Hey! Look!" Ruby smiles, "He's got a snack for me too!"

Ruby smiles when Mr. Shipman sits down and watches TV. Nap time! She lays down and sleeps whiles he works. She dreams of swimming in the pond behind the house! That would be so cool and refreshing! She smiles in her sleep and paddles her arms a little! Swimming is so neat!

Ruby smiles when Mr. Shipman wakes up! It's dinner time and she so excited to see that there more chicken for her to eat up!

Wow ! Life is so good and wonderful, Ruby thinks, as she smiles at Mr. Shipman, and he rubs the happy spot under her neck. He loves her, and she love him! He's such a good Daddy!

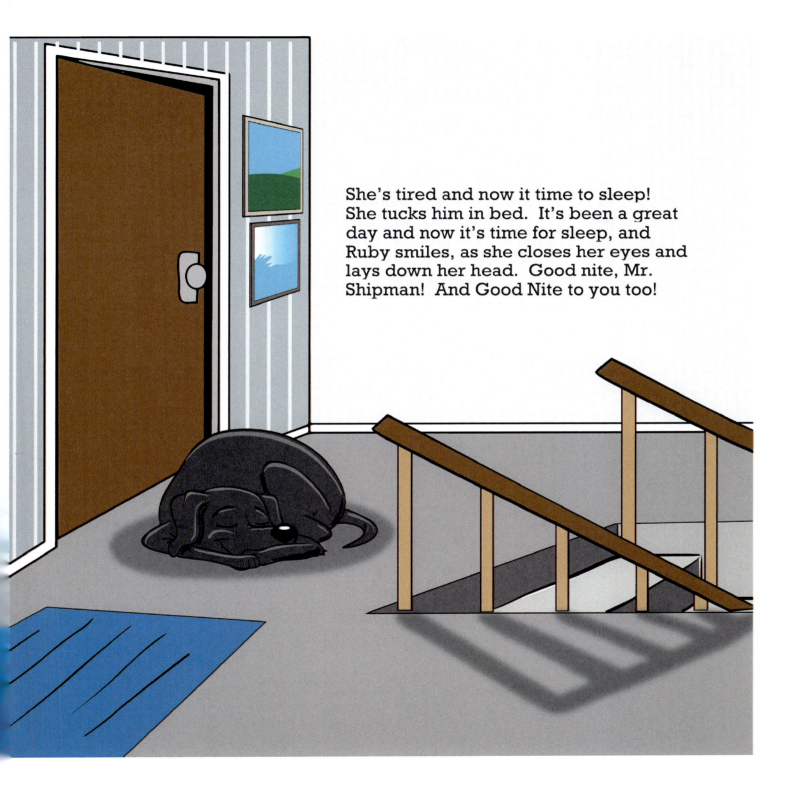

She's tired and now it time to sleep! She tucks him in bed. It's been a great day and now it's time for sleep, and Ruby smiles, as she closes her eyes and lays down her head. Good nite, Mr. Shipman! And Good Nite to you too!

Made in the USA
Middletown, DE
29 April 2021